CRYING FREEMAN

ABDUCTION IN CHINATOWN

D0817096

Viz Graphic Novel

CRYING FREEMAN GRAPHIC NOVEL

ABDUCTION IN CHINATOWN

Story by Kazuo Koike
Art by Ryoichi Ikegami

Translation/Will Jacobs and Matt Thorn
Touch-Up Art & Lettering/Wayne Truman
Cover Design/Viz Graphics
Editors/Satoru Fujii & Trish Ledoux
Executive Editor/Seiji Horibuchi
Publisher/Masahiro Oga

First published by Shogakukan, Inc. in Japan
Editor-in-Chief/Yonosuke Konishi (Shogakukan, Inc.)
Executive Editor/Katsuya Shirai (Shogakukan, Inc.)

Published by Viz Comics
P.O. Box 77010 • San Francisco, CA 94107

10 9 8 7 6 5 4 3 2 1
First Printing August, 1993

ABDUCTION IN CHINATOWN

CRYING FREEMAN GRAPHIC NOVEL

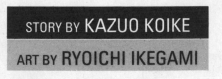

STORY BY **KAZUO KOIKE**

ART BY **RYOICHI IKEGAMI**

CONTENTS

7

NOW IS WHEN THE EVIL SPIRITS FROM HELL RUN AMOK IN THIS WORLD.

DOES THE JAPANESE ANCESTRAL FESTIVAL HAVE ANYTHING TO DO WITH IT?

.....

THEY COME TO THIS WORLD ASTRIDE HORSES MADE OF STRAW...

...BUT RETURN TO THEIR OWN ON COWS.

I UNDERSTAND THAT SPIRITS COME BACK TO THIS WORLD TO SEE THEIR DESCENDANTS DURING THE FESTIVAL.

I'VE HEARD THE SAME STORY.

8

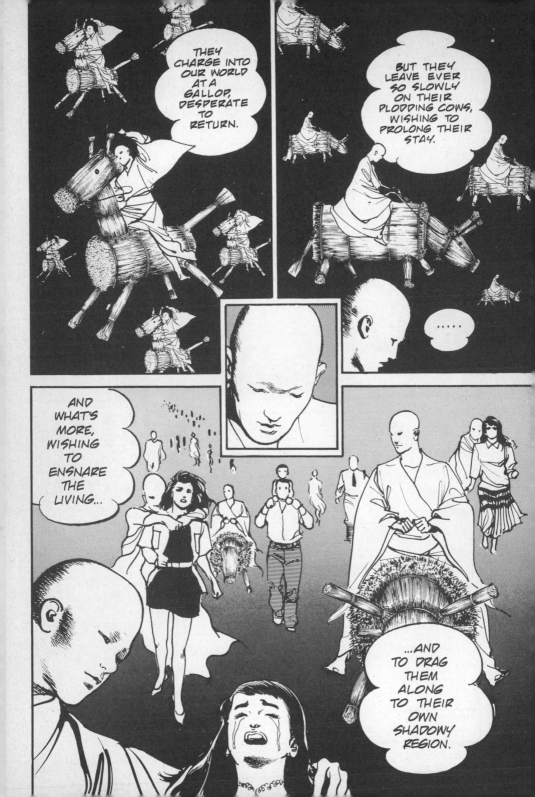

DON'T THEY HAVE A SIMILAR LEGEND IN CHINA?

MERELY A SUPERSTITION.

IT IS SAID THAT THESE SPIRITS SOMETIMES LATCH ONTO PLANES...

...AND SEND THEM PLUMMETING TO EARTH.

.....

RMMMH

EVIL SPIRITS. NO DOUBT HUNDREDS HAVE ME IN THEIR CLUTCHES.

THE SPIRITS OF THE MEN I'VE KILLED...

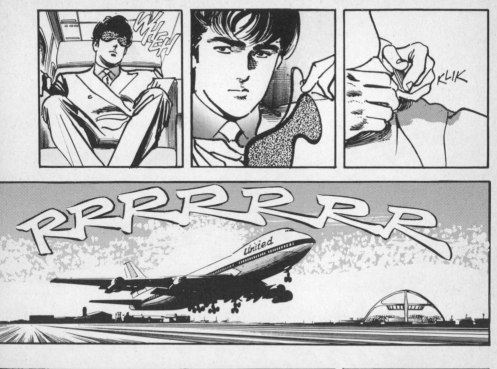

13

THE TIGER CALLS THE WIND, AND HE MAKES THE CLOUD SWELL. THE CLOUD CALLS THE DRAGON, AND HE MAKES THE SUN RISE.

THANK YOU FOR COMING, OM THAI YEUNG!

MY DAUGHTER,
HER HUSBAND,
AND MY
GRANDDAUGHTER
HAVE BEEN
KIDNAPPED.

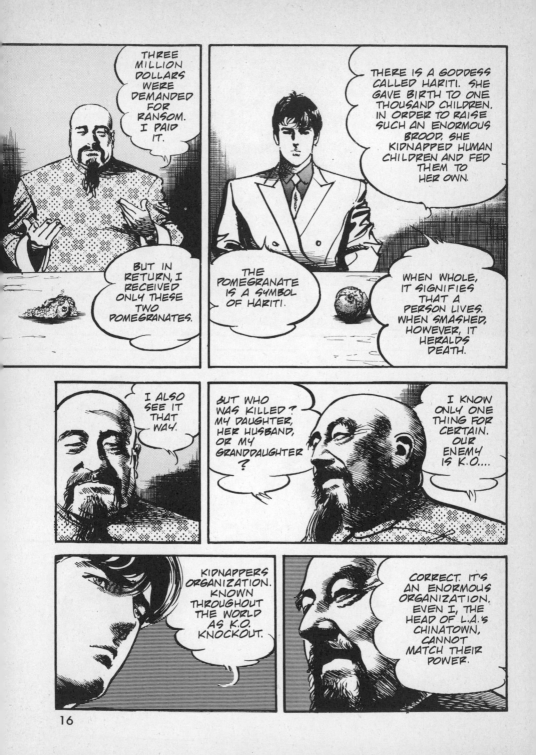

THREE MILLION DOLLARS WERE DEMANDED FOR RANSOM. I PAID IT.

THERE IS A GODDESS CALLED HARITI. SHE GAVE BIRTH TO ONE THOUSAND CHILDREN. IN ORDER TO RAISE SUCH AN ENORMOUS BROOD, SHE KIDNAPPED HUMAN CHILDREN AND FED THEM TO HER OWN.

BUT IN RETURN, I RECEIVED ONLY THESE TWO POMEGRANATES.

THE POMEGRANATE IS A SYMBOL OF HARITI.

WHEN WHOLE, IT SIGNIFIES THAT A PERSON LIVES. WHEN SMASHED, HOWEVER, IT HERALDS DEATH.

I ALSO SEE IT THAT WAY.

BUT WHO WAS KILLED? MY DAUGHTER, HER HUSBAND, OR MY GRANDDAUGHTER?

I KNOW ONLY ONE THING FOR CERTAIN. OUR ENEMY IS K.O....

KIDNAPPERS ORGANIZATION. KNOWN THROUGHOUT THE WORLD AS K.O. KNOCKOUT.

CORRECT. IT'S AN ENORMOUS ORGANIZATION. EVEN I, THE HEAD OF L.A.'S CHINATOWN, CANNOT MATCH THEIR POWER.

17

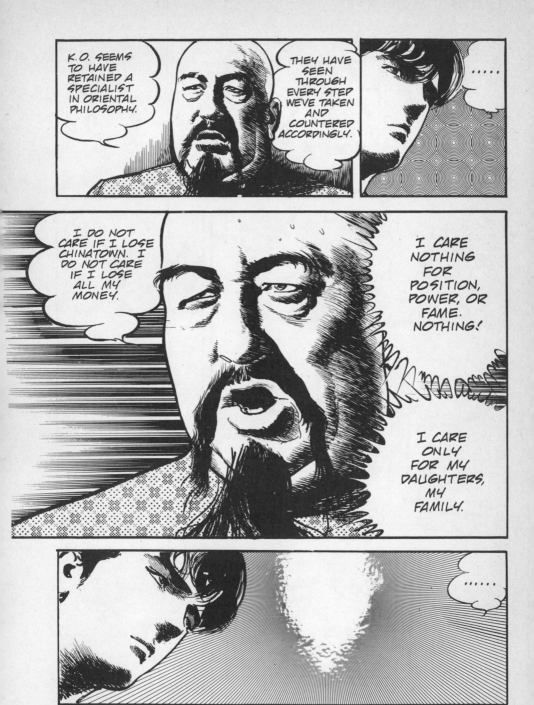

18

19

20

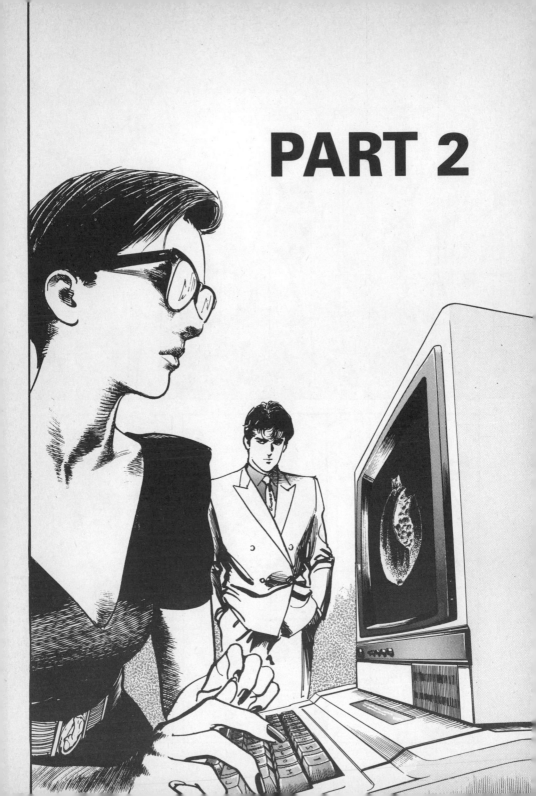

24

25

SSSSS

THE WONG FAMILY HAS BEEN IN CONTROL OF CHINATOWN FOR ALMOST SIXTY YEARS.

WHAT DOES K.O. WANT? IT WOULD AVAIL THEM NOTHING TO TAKE OVER.

THEY WOULD NEVER WIN THE TRUST AND RESPECT OF THE PEOPLE. THEY BELONG TO THE WRONG RACE.

WHITE PEOPLE WOULD STAND OUT HERE.

THIS GROUP, KIDNAPPERS ORGANIZATION, IS FEARED WORLDWIDE.

WHAT COULD THEY WANT FROM WONG?

WONG IS POWERFUL ENOUGH TO SUMMON ME, THE HEAD OF THE 108 DRAGONS.

K.O. MUST KNOW THIS.

I'VE HOOKED UP TO **DAVID**, THE PENTAGON STRATEGY COMPUTER.

RUN A CHECK FOR A RETIRED GREEN BERET.

HE MUST BE WELL-INFORMED IN ORIENTAL PHILOSOPHY AND SYMBOLOGY.

WILL DO.

30

THK

YOU'LL BE OKAY. THE WOUND ISN'T SERIOUS.

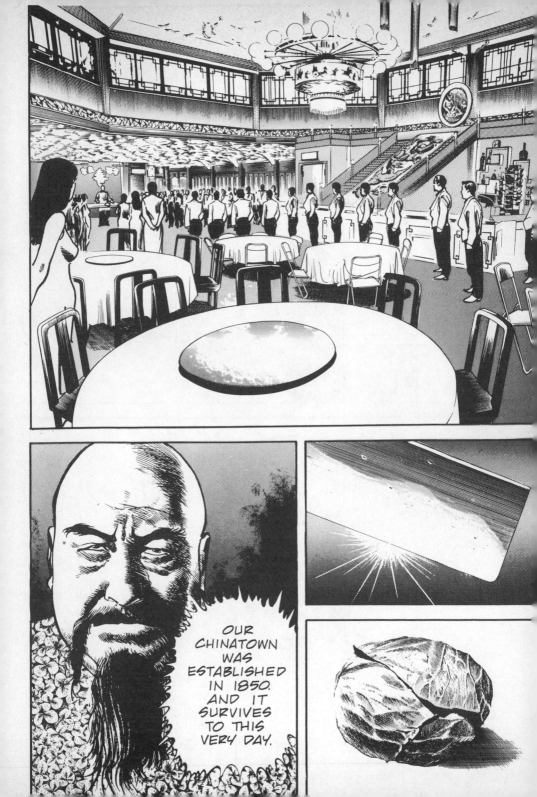

OUR CHINATOWN WAS ESTABLISHED IN 1850. AND IT SURVIVES TO THIS VERY DAY.

THE FIRST BUSINESS TO OPEN HERE WAS A RESTAURANT NAMED CHI PUS.

LEFTOVER LEAVES AND STEMS OF VEGETABLES WERE PURCHASED, SEASONED, AND SERVED. BUT THEIR PRICES WERE CHEAP, SO THEY BECAME VERY POPULAR WITH THE WORKERS.

THAT'S HOW OUR CHINATOWN GOT STARTED.

KRUNCH

WE'VE SURVIVED ALL THESE YEARS IN SPITE OF ANTI-FOREIGN AGGRESSION.

UNITY HAS BEEN THE KEY.

WE HAVE NEVER BETRAYED EACH OTHER.

OUR TOWN HAS ALWAYS MAINTAINED A UNITED FRONT.

THE TRAITOR MUST BE FOUND.

WE MUST FERRET OUT HIS MEANS OF COMMUNICATION.

IF WE SUCCEED IN THIS, WE SUCCEED IN FINDING THE TRAITOR.

KENCH KENCH KENCH KENCH KENCH

THWAK THWAK

NONE OF THE RETIRED GREEN BERETS FITS THE DESCRIPTION.

DITTO FOR THE MEN ON ACTIVE DUTY.

WE CAN'T FIND A COMMUNICATIONS ANTENNA ANYWHERE.

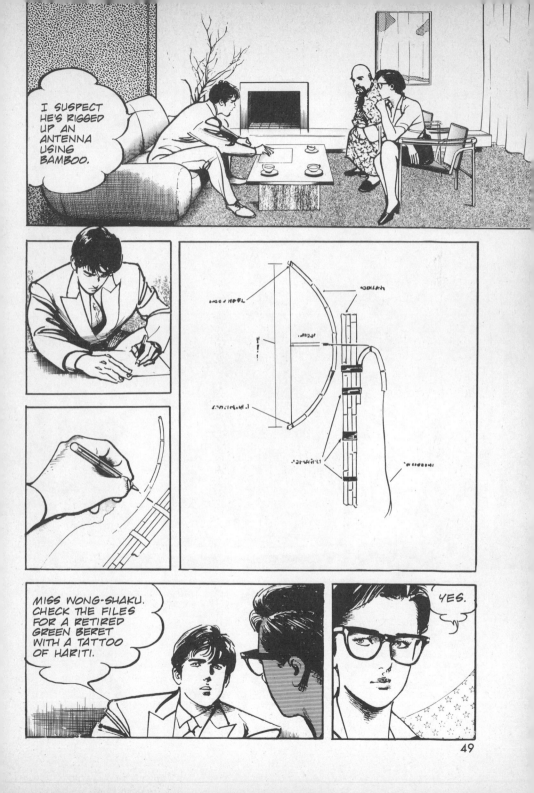

I SUSPECT HE'S RIGGED UP AN ANTENNA USING BAMBOO.

MISS WONG-SHAKU. CHECK THE FILES FOR A RETIRED GREEN BERET WITH A TATTOO OF HARITI.

YES.

AAA

LARRY BUCK.
A FIRST LIEUTENANT
AT THE TIME OF
HIS RETIREMENT.
HE'S AN EXPERT
SKY DIVER, SKIER,
SCUBA DIVER,
AND ROCK
CLIMBER.

HMM. A REAL
PROFESSIONAL.

AN EXPERT SKY DIVER...

WE HAVE LEARNED THAT THE TRAITOR WAS USING BAMBOO AS AN ANTENNA FOR HIS SECRET COMMUNICATIONS.

WE ALSO LEARNED THAT A MAN NAMED LARRY BUCK, A RETIRED GREEN BERET, IS SOMEHOW INVOLVED.

WE'LL PROBABLY HAVE PIECED TOGETHER THE WHOLE STORY BY TOMORROW.

51

WE'VE PUSHED THE TRAITOR TO THE POINT WHERE HE HAS TO CONTACT HIS PEOPLE IMMEDIATELY.

HE WON'T USE THE ANTENNA, NOR THE TELEPHONE.

ALL STREETS AND ALLEYS... EVEN THE SEWERS... ARE BEING CLOSELY WATCHED.

SKY-HOOK.

THAT LEAVES HIM ONLY ONE WAY TO GET OUT OF TOWN.

YES. A TECHNIQUE OFTEN EMPLOYED BY GREEN BERETS.

IT'S TOO DIFFICULT TO EXTRACT A MAN BY HELICOPTER OVER CHINATOWN.

IT WOULD EASILY BE DETECTED AND TRACED BY ITS RADIOWAVES.

DO YOU THINK THEY'LL COME?

CERTAINLY. THEIR C-130 HAS PROBABLY FLOWN OVER THIS AREA FOR SKY-HOOK EVERY NIGHT AT A CERTAIN PREDETERMINED TIME.

THEY WOULD HAVE MADE ARRANGEMENTS TO PICK UP THE TRAITOR IF THE NEED AROSE.

uh

DOES IT HURT?

MY FATHER'S NO LONGER YOUNG, AND HE'S UNDER A LOT OF STRESS. I'VE GOT TO HANG ON.

53

IF I AM THE CAUSE OF YOUR TROUBLE, I INSIST UPON TAKING FULL RESPONSIBILITY.

I'VE BEEN TOLD THAT YOU BEAR THE TATTOO OF THE DRAGON, AND YOUR WIFE THAT OF THE TIGER.

THE WONG FAMILY BEARS THE PHOENIX.

SHH

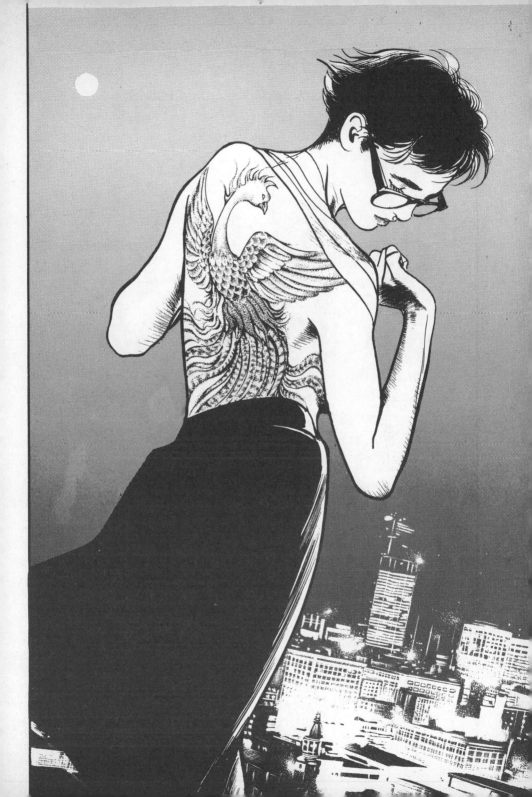

56

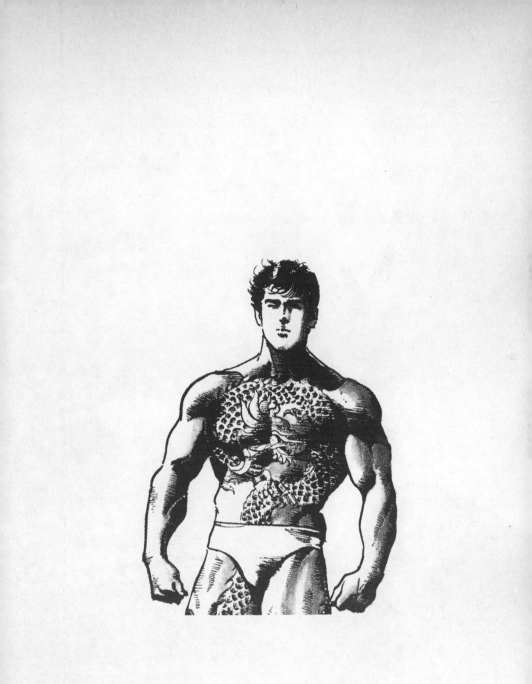

PART 4

SHOOOO

HE'S INFLATING IT WITH HELIUM.

63

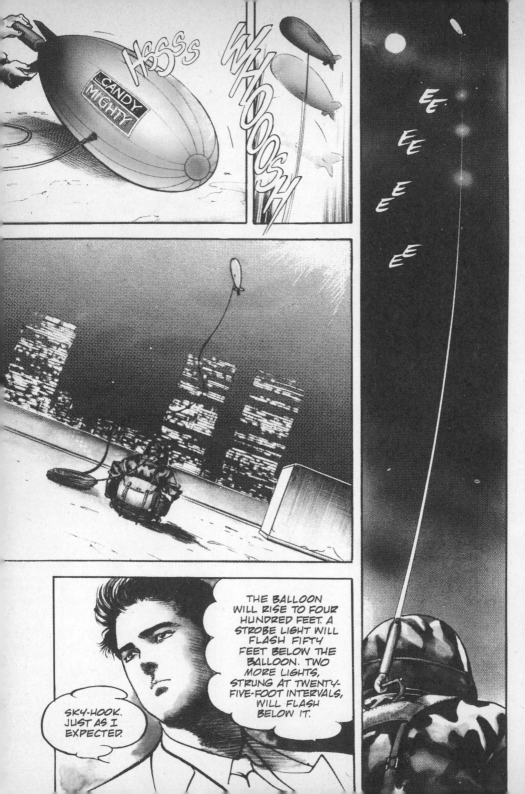

HSSSs

WHOOOSH

EEE
EE
E
EE

CANDY
MIGHTY

THE BALLOON
WILL RISE TO FOUR
HUNDRED FEET. A
STROBE LIGHT WILL
FLASH FIFTY
FEET BELOW THE
BALLOON. TWO
MORE LIGHTS,
STRUNG AT TWENTY-
FIVE-FOOT INTERVALS,
WILL FLASH
BELOW IT.

SKY-HOOK.
JUST AS I
EXPECTED.

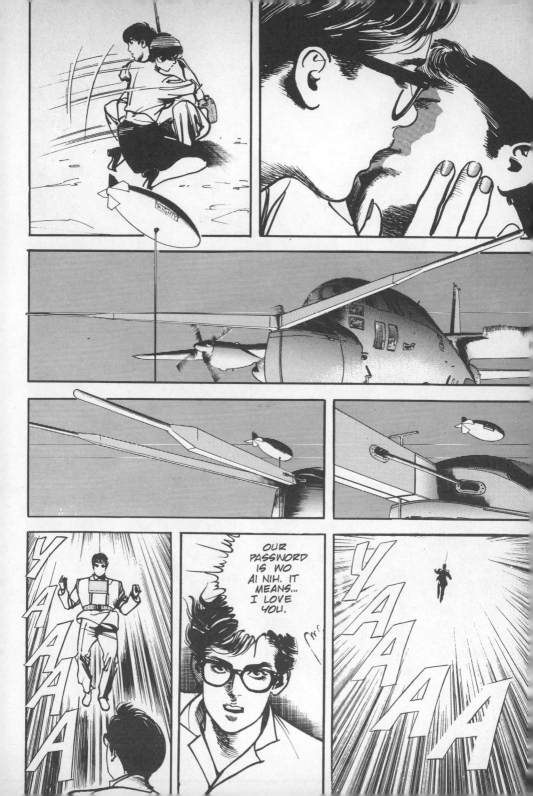

OUR PASSWORD IS WO AI NIH. IT MEANS... I LOVE YOU.

78

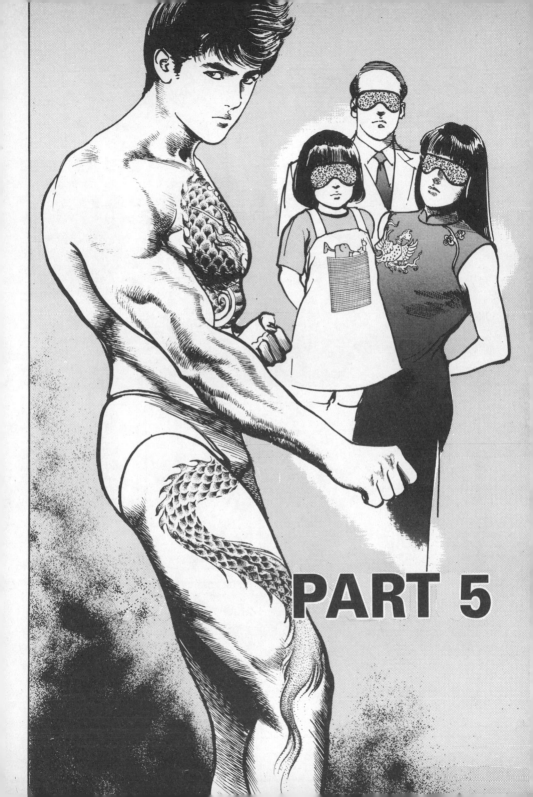

PART 5

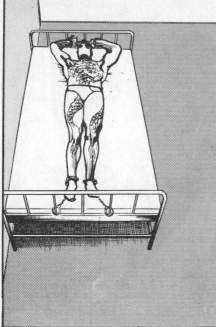

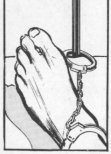

ARE YOU AWAKE, FREEMAN?

I'M BOYD. LUCKY BOYD. HA HA HA HA! PEOPLE CALL ME THAT BECAUSE I'M THE LUCKIEST MAN ALIVE.

YOU CAN CALL ME LUCKY, TOO.

THAT'S AN INCREDIBLE TATTOO.

I FEEL AS IF I'VE CAUGHT A REAL LIVE DRAGON.

WHAT DO YOU WANT?

83

DEPLOY FOR COMBAT.

GRRRR

YES, SIR.

DON'T UNDERESTIMATE US. THIS MAY LOOK LIKE AN ORDINARY CRUISER, BUT WE'RE EQUIPPED LIKE A FRIGATE.

HA HA HA HA HA HA

84

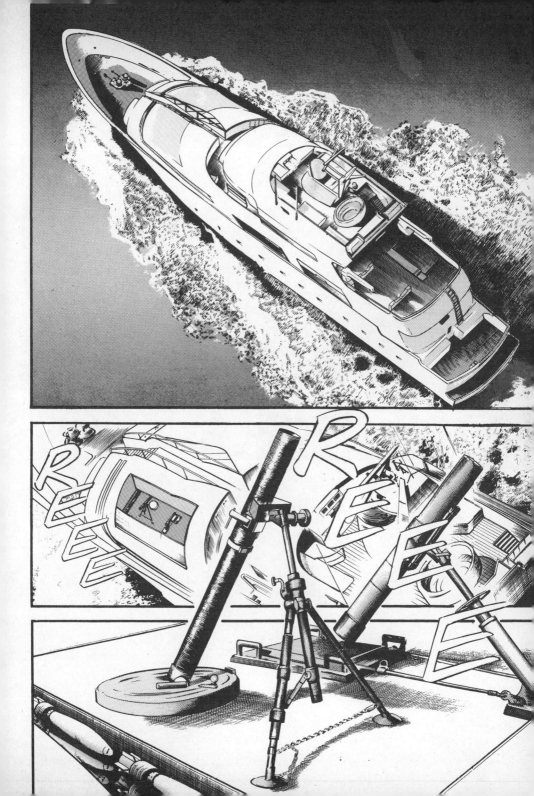

88

90

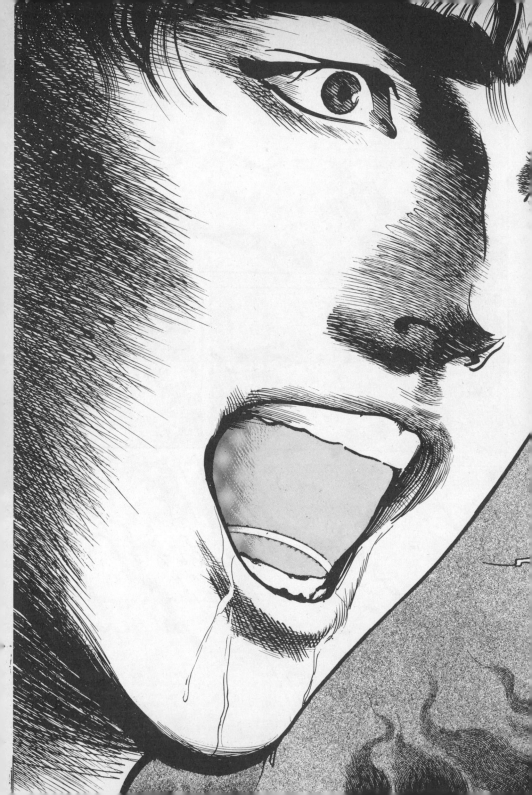

95

99

THE GIRL IS OKAY, BOTH PHYSICALLY AND MENTALLY. BUT HER PARENTS ARE VEGETABLES.

THEY RETAIN ONLY THE INSTINCT OF PARENTAL LOVE.

MMF.

THE WONG FAMILY WON'T RAISE A HAND AGAINST US AS LONG AS WE HAVE THE GIRL.

CONSEQUENTLY, SHE MUST BE WELL CARED FOR.

IT WOULDN'T DO TO HAVE HER GET SICK, OR HURT, OR ANY DAMN THING. SO WE KIDNAPPED HER PARENTS, TOO.

UGH

UGH

UGH

REACH YOUR LIMIT? HA HA HA HA!

THMP

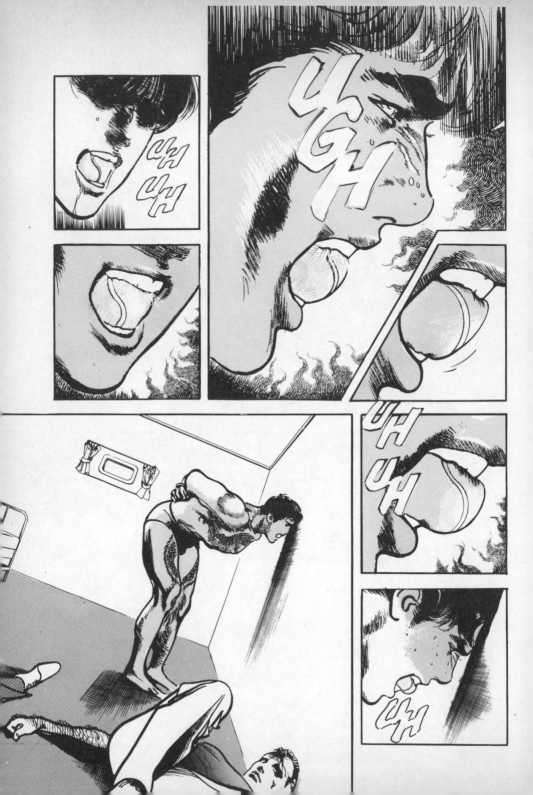

HELLO, BROTHER.

YOU MADE IT ON TIME.

I ALWAYS MAKE IT ON TIME.

113

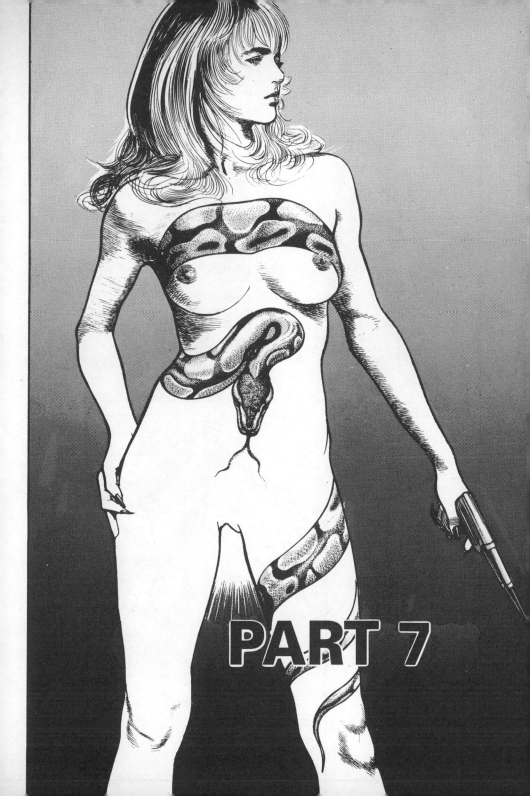

PART 7

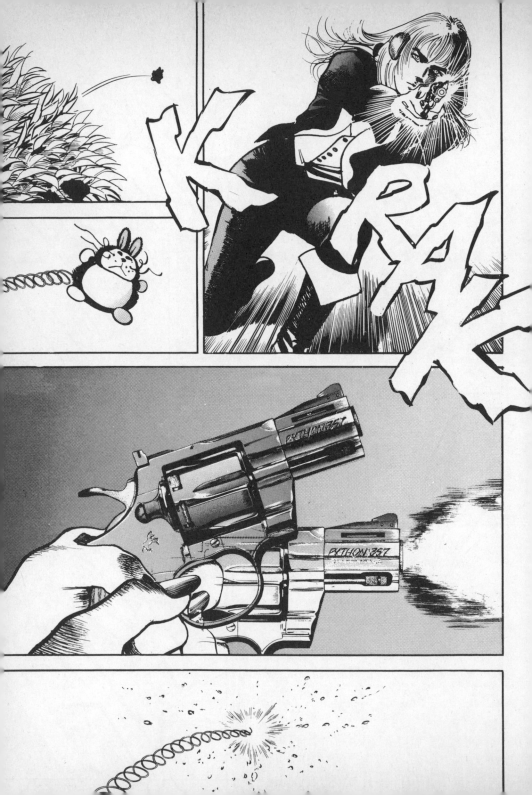

122

IS THIS THE BEST EQUIPMENT THE KIDNAPPERS CAN MUSTER?

THESE EX-GREEN BERETS ARE PRETTY OLD-FASHIONED.

I GUESS THE DRAGON SUBMARINE HASN'T MADE IT THROUGH THE MINE ZONE YET.

127

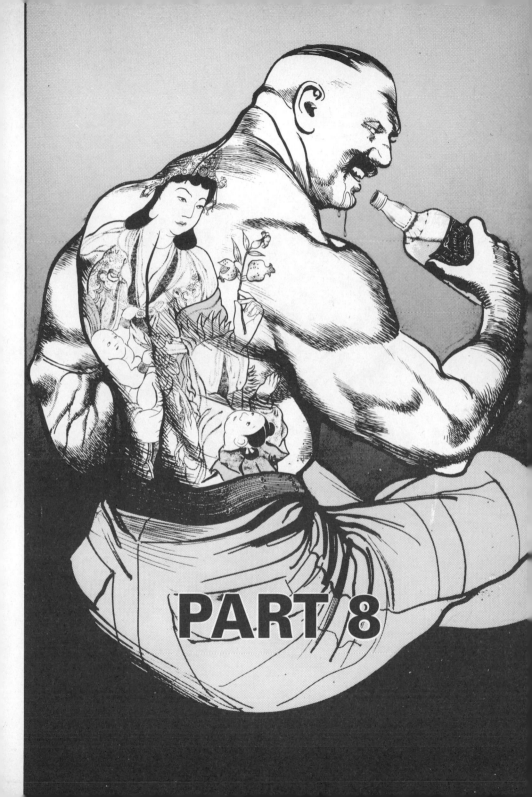

PART 8

142

143

153

YOU HAVE GOOD EQUIPMENT.

YES, WE DO. ALTHOUGH IT'S A BIT OLD-FASHIONED.

164

THAT'S WHY ALL THEIR GOVERNMENTS LEAVE US ALONE. THEIR BENIGN NEGLECT IS THEIR FINAL ACT OF RESPONSIBILITY.

HA HA

HA HA

...

AN AMERICAN, THE FATHER OF AN MIA, BOUGHT US THIS PLACE, ASKING US TO RESCUE HIS SON IN VIET NAM.

THE RELATIVES OF THE OTHER MISSING SOLDIERS KEEP THIS PLACE FUNDED AND SUPPLIED.

TOO BAD, FREEMAN, WE REALLY HAVEN'T GOT A THING AGAINST THE 108 DRAGONS.

...

BUT THESE RAMBOS NEED FORMIDABLE OPPONENTS TO FIGHT AGAINST.

OBVIOUSLY, WE CAN'T DECLARE WAR ON NATIONS. SO WE SQUARE OFF AGAINST PEOPLE LIKE THE MAFIA, THE WONG CLAN, AND YOUR NOTORIOUS ORGANIZATION.

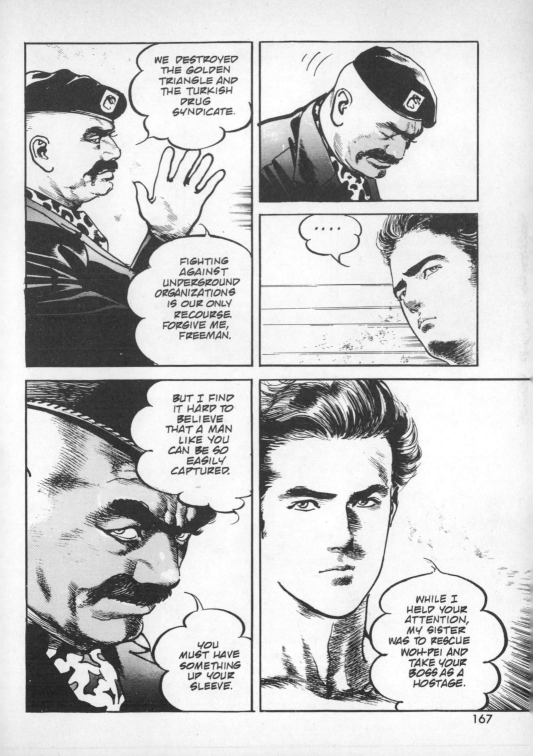

WE DESTROYED THE GOLDEN TRIANGLE AND THE TURKISH DRUG SYNDICATE.

FIGHTING AGAINST UNDERGROUND ORGANIZATIONS IS OUR ONLY RECOURSE. FORGIVE ME, FREEMAN.

....

BUT I FIND IT HARD TO BELIEVE THAT A MAN LIKE YOU CAN BE SO EASILY CAPTURED.

YOU MUST HAVE SOMETHING UP YOUR SLEEVE.

WHILE I HELD YOUR ATTENTION, MY SISTER WAS TO RESCUE WOH-PEI AND TAKE YOUR BOSS AS A HOSTAGE.

167

PART 10

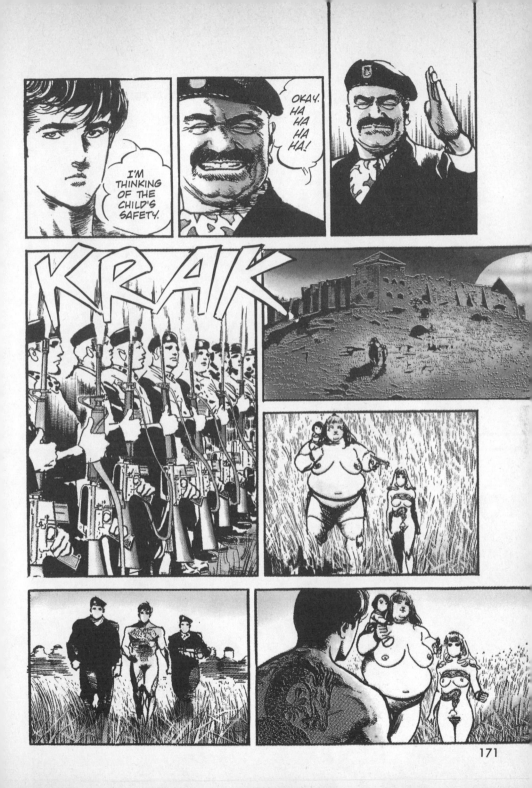

Wha--?

HOW DO YOU LIKE THAT, FREEMAN?

GO AHEAD AND SHOOT HER, IVORY FAN. WE DON'T CARE.

SIGH

I AM SORRY, BROTHER.

IT'S OKAY.

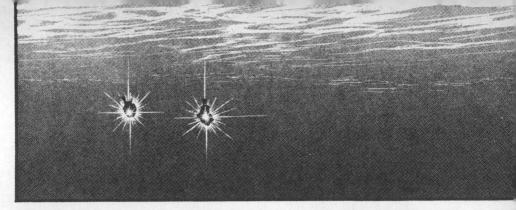

PART 11

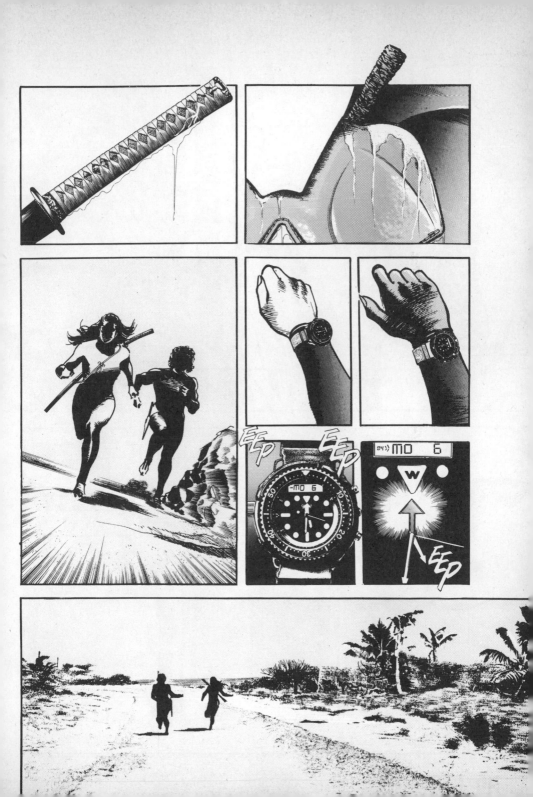

I DIDN'T SAY A WORD TO THE POLICE.

Ohhhh...

I'VE
BEEN
YOUR
SLAVE
EVER
SINCE.

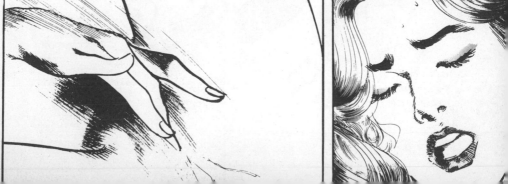

198

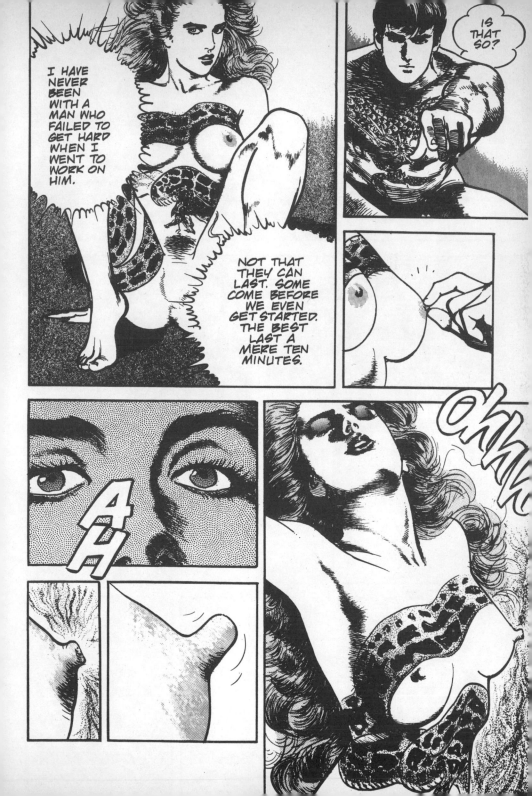

202

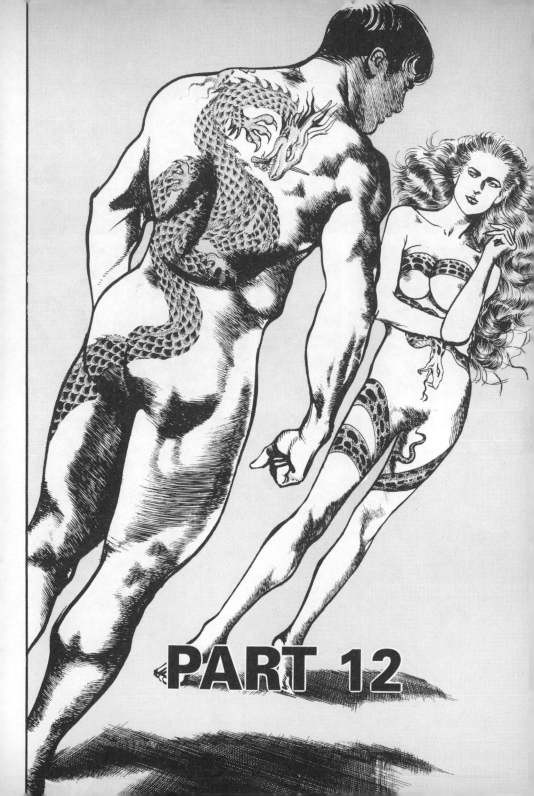

PART 12

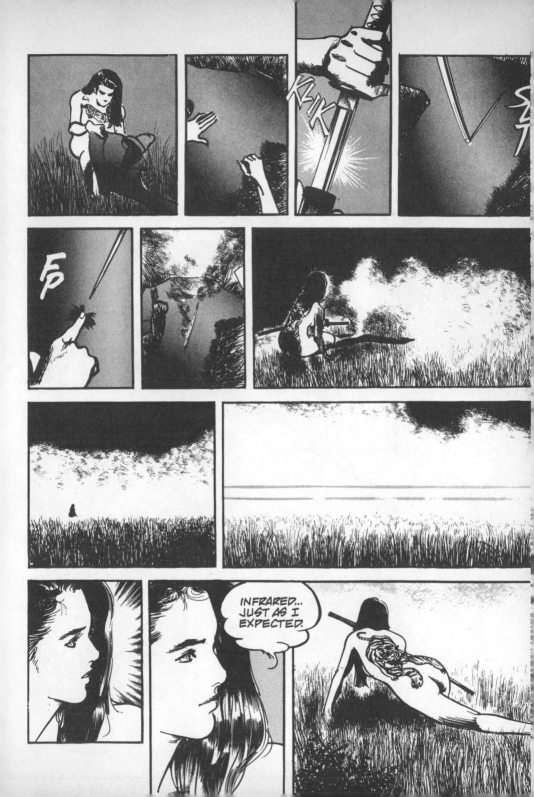

209

210

211

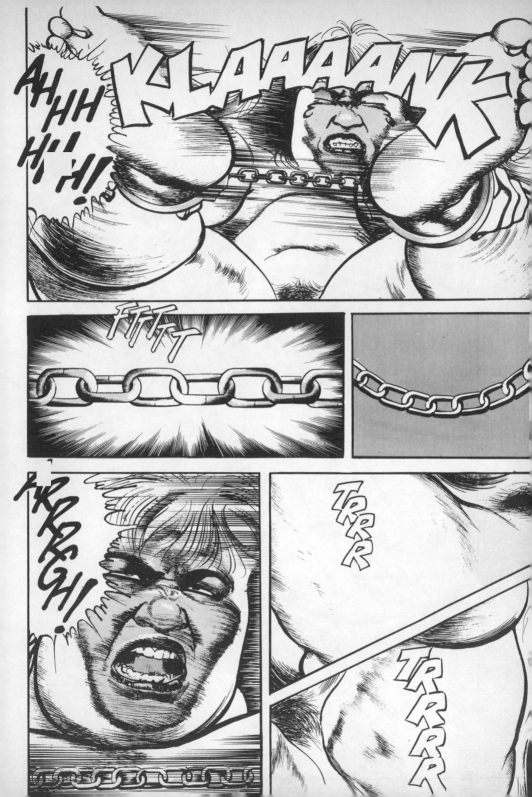

YAH YAH YAH YAH

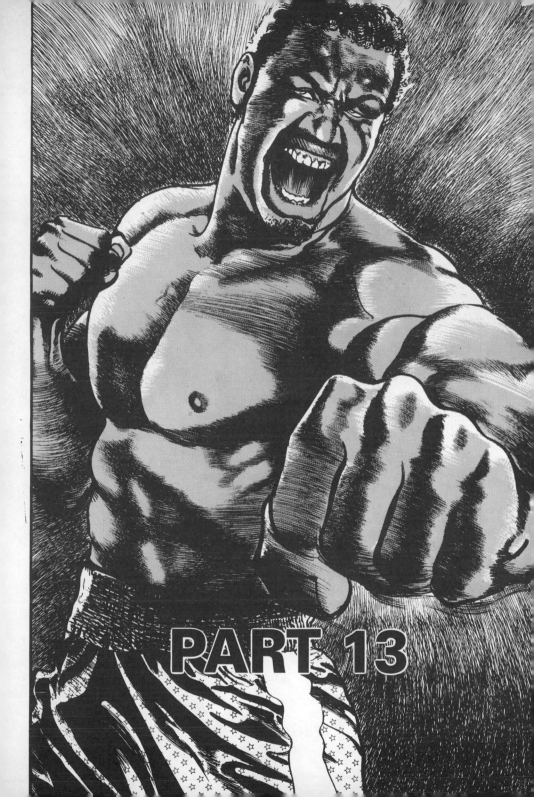

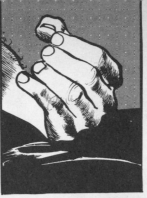

ZPPPPP

FP FP FP FP

WAP WAP

OHHHH

GORDON.
I'LL LET
YOU DO
IT TO ME
IF YOU
WIN!

ARGH HHHHH

230

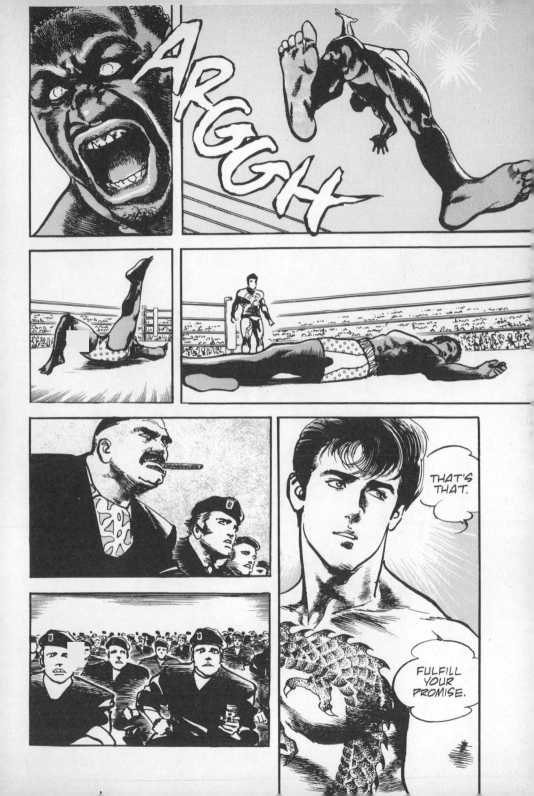

PART 14

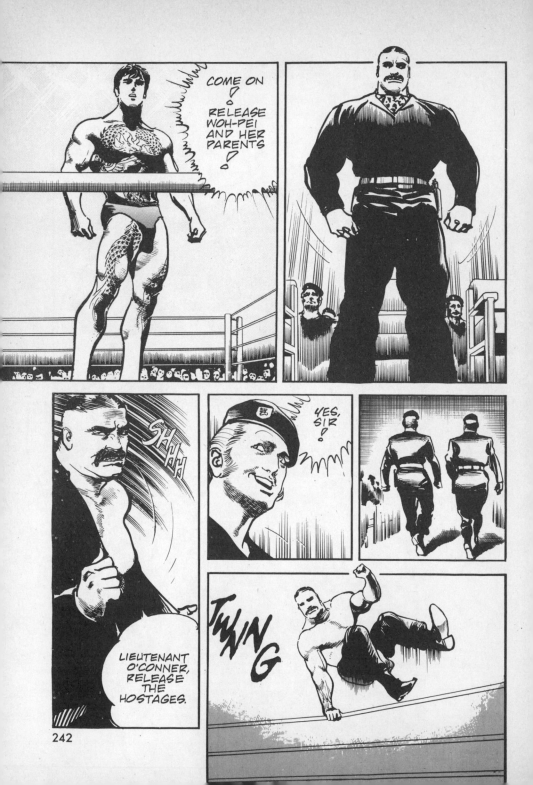

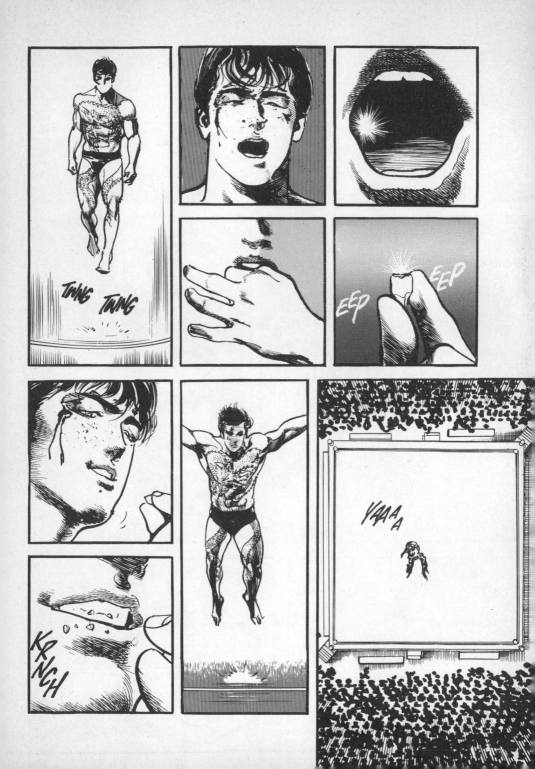

IT STOPPED. MY HUSBAND CAUGHT ON.

IT'S TIME TO ATTACK, IVORY FAN.

ALL RIGHT! LET'S GET 'EM, SISTER!

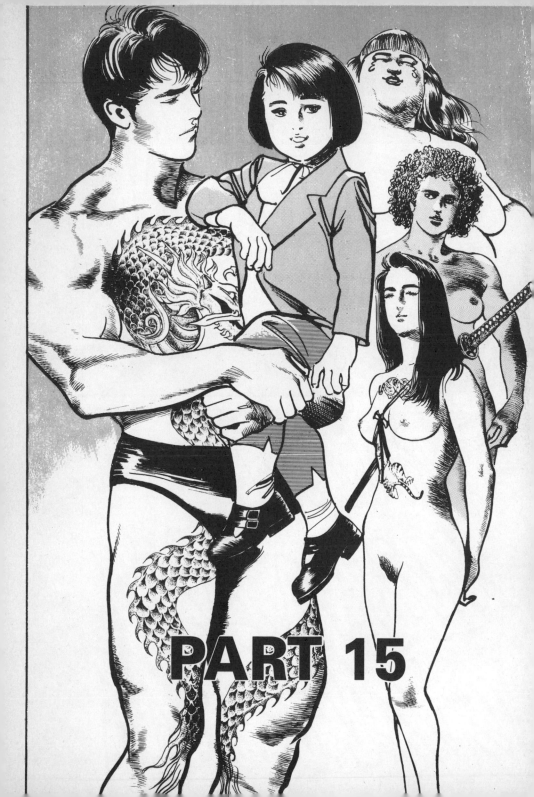

PART 15

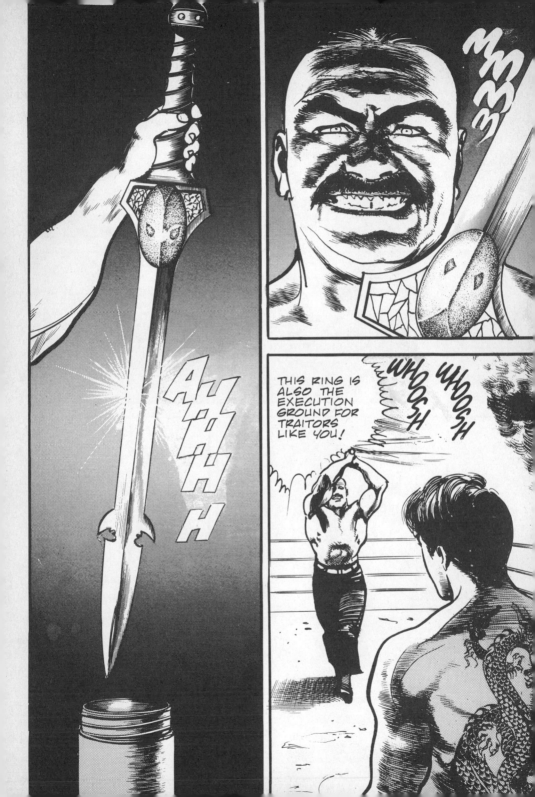

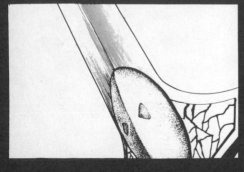

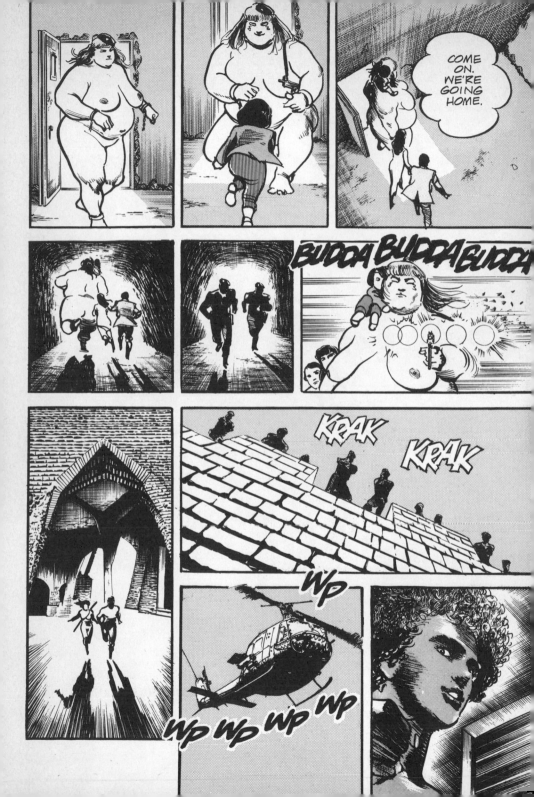

END